The Flea and the Cauliflower

by

John Adrian Talbot Healy

AuthorHouse™ UK Ltd.
500 Avebury Boulevard
Central Milton Keynes, MK9 2BE
www.authorhouse.co.uk
Phone: 08001974150

First published by AuthorHouse 8/11/2009

ISBN: 978-1-4490-1360-8 (sc)

This book is printed on acid-free paper.

authorHOUSE®

Dedicated To The Memory Of Rosemary.

PREFACE

Before you read this short story, you must place your mind into an imaginary, and tiny world of the insect, or Entomology, as some people would prefer it to be called.

Assemble your own thoughts, with pictures in your mind, as no amount of written words can compete with the visions of the brain. You can create more in your head than I could ever put down on paper. To read this story does help to build a complete fantasy.

INTRODUCTION

This is the story of a tiny flea called Fergus. He lived in comfort on a large dog called Maxamillion. The good life ends abruptly when he is forced from his canine host, and ends up inside a giant cauliflower. This was the beginning of a great adventure for Fergus. He twice escapes being eaten alive by enormous predators. Poor old Fergus then nearly starves to death, but survives this, only to discover a complete living village within the confines of this giant vegetable.

Fergus ends up fighting for the love of his life. He is the groom of a very lively wedding, and becomes the father of triplets.

Our little hero, and his family witness the destruction of the entire village. A new life begins on the ground for the Fergus family with many more adventures. They meet a friendly, and very helpful giant worm called Willie. Then there is the beautiful butterfly called Laurali, who takes them all on a flight of fancy, and I must not forget the assistance of a squadron of helpful fireflies.

A complete circle happens for Fergus, when he eventually returns to live on Maximillion with his complete family. He is also joined by the entire inhabitants from the old village. Their aim was to start a new and blissful future. But first we must return to the time when Fergus was born.

Let the story begin.

CHAPTER 1

The Teenage Years

Once, up, on a thyme leaf, Fergus the flea was born. He was one of a very large family who saw the light of day on this thyme leaf. Fergus, and all his friends had to bide their time until some sort of animal passed by the thyme bush, and sure enough along came Maxamillion, Max for short, a large shaggy dog. He looked more like a wise, sly hairy fox than a dog. Just as he trotted towards the thyme plant the ambush was imminent.

When the dog was directly below, the group jumped together. Just like a band of paratroopers they silently dropped on poor old Max, without their chutes of course. It was just like an army of invaders. Max did not even feel them land. The group quickly dispersed throughout the dog's fur. They knew that from now on they would have breakfast, lunch, and dinner as fleas lived mostly on the blood of animals. The victim was poor old Max. He was their unwilling host.

Fergus, the flea, lived happily with all his tiny friends on Max. This dog was now their playground, and he was not very happy about it. All he seemed to do all day long was feel irritable. This, of course, was due to the large amount of inhabitants now dwelling on his body. They were all the time, running, skipping, hopping, and jumping, which annoyed the poor old dog immensely. Max was slowly being driven mad.

These tiny insects had arrived on Max as minors. It was not very long before they had reached their teens. Fergus, and many of his friends, were orphans. They were clothed, and fed by the elders of the colony. A blood bank was set up for such hungry waifs. They were extremely glad of this service.

These kids behaved just like all other youngsters. Some were tearaways, and hooligans. Others were model children. Fergus was placed somewhere in the middle of all these categories. He was young, slim, tall, and handsome with deep blue eyes, and long eye lashes. With these looks, he could not help being a bit of a flirt. Fergus wore a suit of many colours, each leg was of a different hue, and to top it all, the hat was black to match his two pairs of brogue shoes. This was finished off with a pair of fancy black shiny gloves that reached up to his elbows. He did look extremely dapper.

Fergus was always having lots of fights. Some he won, and some he lost. There were some small romances, which only led to the pain of a broken heart. It was all part of the process of growing up. Fergus was a very popular figure amongst all his little friends. Our hero had a particular friend called Dwiddle. They were always getting up to all sorts of mischief. Like playing tricks on older fleas and running away. There was one time when they tied a very thin dog hair across a well used path. Every day adult fleas would be walking along this path happily chatting to each other. They would not notice the trip wire, or hair, as it really was, and then it was too late. They would go flying head over heels, and possibly break a leg or two, or maybe even three. Usually the culprits were the scallywags known as Fergus, and Dwiddle. They would be hiding nearby, and would roar with laughter. They then would run away sniggering. It was great fun for them, but not for the poor old victims, they were the ones that really suffered.

Fergus, and his friends used to play a dangerous game called swinging out. They would choose the longest dog hair, and swing out like a gorilla. He who swung out the furthest was the hero of the day, and would be admired by all the teenage females. One single dog hair was like a giant rope to a tiny flea.

One day Fergus, in his usual showing off mood, chose a longer than normal hair. He swung out too far, and was now hanging from the underbelly of Maximillion. This was a very frightful experience for Fergus, because he was now dangling from a very thin hair, which could have broken at any moment. He dare not let go, he knew that if he lost his grip, his life would end far below on the hard rocky ground. This ground looked miles away to this tiny being. He would have broken every bone in his tiny body if he had fallen.

Fergus just hung there like Tarzan, a jungle character he had once heard about from one of his little friends. He would have to rest for a while in order to regain his strength. This he did, and when he was fully recovered, he started the long haul back to the top of Max. To make things worse, his host started to trot, making the climb even more difficult. The long hair started to bounce with every step Max took.

Eventually, a very worn out Fergus reached the top. It took him three long days to do it. All his tiny friends were delighted to see his head appear from the depths to which he had fallen. He cried out for help. They all rushed to his aid, and hauled him up the last little bit to safety. Fergus was grateful for this, as he had no strength left in his worn out body.

His friends thought they had lost him for ever, but they could not stop laughing at his folly. Never again will I be so stupid, thought Fergus. From this whole adventure he had learned a serious lesson that would never be forgotten. He was so glad to be back where he belonged, with all his friends. Fergus just lay there looking up at the smiling, and laughing faces of all his rescuers. He felt such a fool, but at least he was now safe.

CHAPTER 2

Social Evenings

Fergus had the misfortune of never knowing his mother or father. Slowly this pain was eased by the companionship of the large number of brothers, sisters, and many friends. They all looked after each others needs.

This group would all meet every evening just to have a social gathering. Games were played, popular songs were sung, and little innocent childhood love affairs developed.

CHAPTER 3

Day Of The Rains

One day Max was running along a well used path. Suddenly the heavens opened, the rain fell for hours with such violence. Max got soaked to the skin. He loved this wet feeling as it kept his little on board inhabitants very inactive, it was just like having a shower. Maxamillion felt great.

With this torrential downpour, it did not take long for Max to get saturated. He started to shake violently in order to get rid of all the rain water gathering in his fur. This sudden shaking caught poor old Fergus by surprise. It was like an earthquake. He tried to grab hold of a dog hair but could not hang on. Eventually after rolling and tumbling for some time he managed to grab a single hair. The dog's shaking grew more and more violent. Fergus screamed for help, but no one was there.

Eventually Fergus got so weak that he had to let go of the dog hair. He shot straight out of Max's fur, and upwards toward the sky. He saw the ground shrink as he went higher, and higher. This poor little flea was terrified.

CHAPTER 4

A Strange New World

Fergus floated for some time on the blustery wind. He felt like a spaceman who was looking down on the earth. Soon he began to lose height. He was now heading back towards the ground with great speed. Fergus crash landed on the top of a giant cauliflower. The surface was so large, he could not see any horizon on this sphere. He felt as if he was on the moon.

Just as he hit the top of the cauliflower he rolled over a few times, and fell straight into a small opening in one of the florets of the large vegetable. Fergus was in pain.

Down and down he drifted into a strange white world. All around him he saw what looked like gigantic white trees that went on, and on. These of course were enormous cauliflower florets. Fergus did not know what they were, as he had spent most of his life on a dog. He really believed he was on another planet.

This was quite scary for Fergus. He wished some of his friends were there to support him, at least they would have shared his terror of the unforeseen. He had no one to turn to. He was completely alone.

After falling for some time Fergus eventually hit a ledge near the floor of the cauliflower. He banged his head. This knocked him unconscious. Fergus was out cold. The limp body of our poor old hero just lay prone. He looked as if he was dead.

Two days had elapsed, and still Fergus had not moved. As he lay there his small body jerked, as if he was dreaming. This jerking motion caused him to roll over, and fall straight off the ledge on to the floor of the cauliflower.

Fergus just lay there, dazed, bruised, and battered. His brain was in turmoil. "Where am I?," he screamed. He did not want to move. His eyes were still shut tight. He was afraid to open them.

Suddenly there was a very loud clicking noise from behind him. This was very frightening for Fergus. He now had to open his eyes, and what he saw was a very large beetle bearing down on him with two enormous snapping pincers, similar to that of a crab. Fergus was so scared he just froze, totally unable to move.

 The beetle approached with such a grating noise from his scary claws. These weapons on the beetle could have chopped him in half with just one squeeze, and that would have been the demise of poor old Fergus. He tried to move his legs, but to no avail. Just when he thought that this was the end the beetle went straight past him, and disappeared around one of the cauliflower floret. It vanished as quickly as it had appeared.

Suddenly the legs of Fergus came to life. He was off like a racing car. He was looking for a hiding place. There were not many nooks or crannies to dive into, but he soon found a little cover. Fergus vanished into thin air with great haste, and immediately went into silent mode. This gave him time to evaluate the situation. It was not until now that Fergus realized he had lost all of his beautiful clothes. He was naked except for a small white toga around his waist. This was good for Fergus, as his highly colourful clothes would have easily been spotted by the hungry beatle. He wondered where his suit had vanished to. He thought it was probably ripped off as he was violently thrown out of Max. Later, Fergus was very lucky to find his lost clothing scattered around the area. He quickly dressed himself.

CHAPTER 5

The Hunger

Fergus breathed a sigh of relief. The only reason he survived the attention of the monster beetle, thought Fergus, was that, as he had not eaten for three days, and his main diet was a drop of blood from the blood bank on Maxamillion. He had turned pure white. He was now totally anaemic.

Fergus was looking more like a grain of rice with, legs, arms, and a head. He was the same colour as the white ivory flesh of the cauliflower. This was camouflage at its best, the beetle had not even seen him. The strange three day hunger seemed to have saved our hero's life. For this quirk of nature Fergus was thankful.

He was now desperately in need of food. He wandered aimlessly looking for any morsel to eat. Giant cauliflower florets, and large caverns of the vegetable seemed to go on, and on for ever, casting haunting shadows throughout. The whole place looked eerie. Fergus was getting weaker. He was very scared of these ghostly shadows.

It seemed as if weeks had passed. He was so hungry. "What am I going to do?", said Fergus to himself. He wondered where he was. Poor old Fergus felt lost. He was very near the point of giving up. He knew He just had to keep going.

CHAPTER 6

The Monster Of The Pool

Eventually, Fergus came across small pools of trapped water on the floor of the cauliflower. This water would keep him alive for some time to come. He knew that his small body could not survive for long without water, or some sort of moisture, so he was pleased to see these pools. He ran to one of them and started drinking and gulping the liquid down as if there was no tomorrow.

As Fergus was drinking this precious life saving water, he became aware of a pair of very bright raging red eyes, staring at him from the watery depths of the pool. These eyes did not look very friendly, in fact, they looked extremely menacing. This startled Fergus very badly.

All of a sudden a terrible pair of jaws rose from out of the water. The jaws were full of razor-sharp ugly teeth. They were just about to bite him in half, and swallow this young flea completely.

Fergus's was now getting used to danger, he was now ready for anything. Fergus quickly stood up. His rear legs were like coiled springs. He released the tension in both of them at the same time. He shot straight over the hungry predator's head towards the far side of the pool.

Fergus did not quite make it to the other side, and landed in the shallow part of the water. He looked back, and to his horror, he saw the pool monster was following him with great haste. It was still grinding those awful sharp teeth. Luckily, Fergus was able to stand in the shallow water. He quickly recoiled his rear legs. This time they were more powerful, and once more he released this stored up energy in both of his elastic leg joints. He shot straight out of the pool and well away from his enemy's reach.

Fergus managed to look back, only to see his attacker was now being attacked by what looked like a water spider. It was twice the size of the pool monster. The predator was now the prey. Thank God thought Fergus. He did not want to hang around. He ran like the wind, and disappeared around a giant floret.

There was no way any hungry predator could ever catch him now. Fear gave him this extra strength. He had the determination to survive, otherwise our poor old hero would no longer exist. He was not sure if it was the spider that had saved him, or his elastic legs, but he did not care. He was still alive.

When Fergus thought he was far enough away from danger he stopped running. It was then that he realised he still had not had any food, he was even weaker now. Fergus was now only able to limp, but still had the will to keep on going. Being alone did not help. "What next", he said, as he dropped to his knees, and looked around the empty cavernous cauliflower. All he saw was a great perilous void. It was the silience that nearly drove him mad. He did not know whether to turn left or right, every thing looked the same. It was just like a maze.

CHAPTER 1

The Village

All of a sudden Fergus heard laughter and singing from behind a large clump of florets. He approached with caution, and slowly peered around these florets. Fergus was amazed, and delighted with what he saw. He thought he was looking at a mirage.

What Fergus saw was a complete village, with whole families of insects, all laughing, singing, and dancing. Everybody was looking extremely happy. It was just like a scene from a fairy tale book, but this vision was no fairy tale. In fact, to our heroes delight, it was a welcome vision of reality.

Fergus thought they looked very friendly, so with great difficulty he crawled slowly towards them hoping for help. The moment the villagers saw Fergus, they rushed out to help him. He was carried to the village square where they sat him down. Up to now he was feeling slightly nervous. This feeling soon disappeared with all the attention he was getting.

Fergus was warmly greeted by the leader of the village. He was called Manny, he had one hundred children. Fifty boys, and fifty girls. Manny, was a very appropriate name for the amount of kids he had. His full name was Manny La Rue.

Manny was a fine looking being that radiated a warm personality. He stared at this thin puny little creature for a few moments, and with a big sigh said, "You look absolutely terrible my boy, have you been attacked by something. We must have a good look at you".

The whole village had now gathered around Fergus. They were all hoping to help in any way that they could.

Fergus looked a terrible sight, he seemed worn out, scrawny, and hungry. Manny, and some of his friends started to examine him They found no breaks or wounds on his frail body. The tiny group of rescuers decided that all he needed was food, warmth and rest. The elders covered him with heavy clothing. This made him feel better already.

Manny's wife, prepared some food for him. Fergus thought it tasted good. "What sort of food is this?" he inquired, "its delicious. I have never tasted anything like it". "Oh", said Manny's wife, "It's just cauliflower. We have an endless supply. I cook it in lots of different ways, everybody loves it". Mrs La Rue was very was proud of her culinary skills. Fergus had just become a vegetarian.

After six or seven days of loving tender care, nursing, and devotion from Mrs La rue, Fergus soon recovered from his loss of weight. At last he was now beginning to get back to normal, he could not believe his luck.

He sat there thinking. What is this place? Heaven, no, you have to be dead to go there. Maybe it's Shangrila, a mythical place in people's minds where nobody ever grows old, and everyone is always happy. No, no, was the next thought. This is no dream, this is factual, and he loved everything about it.

CHAPTER 8

A Feeling Of Belonging

Fergus told his new found friends all about his adventures. They listened to his stories, with ears, eyes, and mouths open wide. He told them all about his best friend Dwiddle, and the pranks they got up to. He told them what it was like living on a dog. Fergus let them know what happened when Max started to shake the rain from his coat, and his journey out of Max, and upwards toward the sky. Then there was the banging of his head when he fell into the crevice on the surface of the cauliflower.

Next there came the tale of the large noisy crab like beetle that missed out on a meal by walking straight past him, He recalled the monster predator thing, lurking in the depths of the pool, from which he barely escaped death. He also mentioned the water spider that unknowingly saved his life. They all found these tales very exciting, as life in a cauliflower could sometimes be a little boring. They thought Fergus was some sort of a hero. The stories he told were of great entertainment, and everybody listened intensely. Tales like these were rare, and always had the group spellbound.

Fergus felt like a schoolteacher surrounded by all his little attentive pupils, they followed him everywhere, and wanted more and more stories. Eventually these tales of the adventures of our hero would run out, so he had to make up a few white lies. These were harmless lies. But they did keep everybody happy.

Lots of happy days followed. Fergus was eagerly accepted into the community. He was such a dynamic character. Everywhere he went, people would make such a fuss of him. He was extremely loved by everybody. Our little Hero had become a pillar of society within the village.

CHAPTER 9

The Fight

Fergus had his eye on one particular daughter of Mrs La Rue, her name was Madeleine, or Maddy for short. He was in love, he could not take his eyes off her. She also thought the world of him, after all, he was young, slim, tall and handsome. They were a perfect match for each other.You cannot keep lovers apart.

All was not well in the village. A young suitor of Maddy was very jealous of Fergus. He waved his arms, and challenged Fergus for the love of Manny's beautiful daughter. His name was Mac, Flea. He jumped to his feet and flew at Fergus with a terrible rage in his eyes. He was frothing at the mouth as he lunged at his enemy, both pairs of arms, and legs were flying, and thrashing in the air. Fergus was taken by surprise. He turned quickly to defend himself, and started to wrestle with Mac, Flea.

They looked like two suits of armour locked in deadly combat. The crowd that had gathered looked on in awe, they were scared, and were not used to this sort of violence. Manny, who was large in stature rushed forward and jumped in between them, pushing both apart. He then roared at the top of his voice, "Stop this brawling at once, we do not allow this sort of behaviour in our village. It could cause bloodshed, this is a peaceful community. We never have any trouble in this village, and we want it kept that way".

The fight stopped immediately. The opponents moved apart from each other. But the glaring still continued, the hatred would not go away. Manny spoke again "You must obey our laws, you will sort out your disagreement by simple arm, and leg wrestling. A date will be set aside for the contest". Manny and the other elders talked it over, and after much deliberation, they said the duel would be held two days hence. Maddy would not be allowed to see either suitor until the day of the contest. This would drive the two suitors quite mad, as they both loved her so much, but what could they do?.

The set day duly arrived for the contest. A small circle had already been roped off in the village square. All the village inhabitants gathered around this small makeshift ring. They all were having great expectations of a good mornings wrestling, and to add to this, it was all free.

Just after midday, the two contestants arrived to thunderous applause. It was like a medieval jousting contest scene, with the crowd all looking smart in their Sunday attire. To make it look even better, there were lots of red, green, and yellow flags all around the tiny jousting ring. Little tiny stalls were set up in order to sell food, trinkets, and mementos of this great exciting day, everything looked so colourful. It would be a day to remember.

Maddy was allowed to watch the fight from a distance, she was all tensed up from the fear that her lover might be injured. She shouted to her champion to be careful. This was a dark day for her, and she wished it would end quickly with a favourable outcome.

The combatants could not wait to get at each other, the venom in their eyes was all caused by the love of Maddy. They could not help it, this is a primitive reaction suffered by all living creatures. You can not fight a natural feeling called jealousy.

The referee ordered them both into the ring, and bring their heads together, cheek to cheek. They were then ordered to stand tall on their hind legs, and grasp their opponent's left hand tightly. The next thing they were told was, that when they heard the whistle blow, they should push with all their strength. The first contestant to throw his opponent over his head would be declared the winner.

They stood in the ring waiting for the whistle to blow. It seemed like an eternity . Each could feel the hot breath from his opponent's mouth on his right ear. It was awful. This was a very close contact joust with no quarter given.

Suddenly the whistle blew, the shrill sound of the noise that filled the air was ear piercing. This was the cue to start. Both opponents pushed at the same time. Their strength was equal, neither moved. Fergus tried to push harder but still nothing happened. He just had to win this contest or lose the love of his life. This would be a tragedy for him.

After some time had elapsed there was total stalemate. The crowd were unusually silent, no excitement was happening for them. You could hear a pin drop. Fergus suddenly had a brain wave. He realised that if Mac, Flea had nothing to push against, he could use his opponents strength against him. There was no time to waste. Fergus had to react immediately.

Fergus suddenly unhinged the joints in his knees, this caused him to immediately drop to the ground. The sudden action caught Mac, Flea by surprise, as he was now pushing against nothing. He flew clean over Fergus's head, and into the cold dark depths of the village pond.

Fergus was the champ. There was lots of applause from the crowd. Maddy ran to him, she could not help it. They embraced, and kissed gently, it was a touching moment. But where was Mac, Flea. It seems he had vanished under the water. Some time had elapsed since he disappeared.

The crowd feared he had drowned, but, they were all very pleased to see his head eventually surface from the depths of the pond. He was covered in pond weed as he slowly crawled out of the pool. He was looking very wet, and dishevelled.

 Mac, Flea shook himself dry just like a drenched dog, and when he had finished this shaking, he limped towards the happy couple. Fergus feared there would be more trouble. But he was wrong. Mac, Flea offered his hand in friendship. Fergus reached out, and shook it gladly, they then had a little hug of friendship. Mac, Flea then wished them both well.

A large crowd had now gathered around them, and they showed their approval by loudly clapping. The two enemies became the best of friends from that time on. All three held hands. Maddy, and Fergus had another little embrace, and more applause followed. The whole village was now celebrating. Fergus said to Maddy, " We should get married," She agreed ,but told him that he must get permission from her father.

CHAPTER 10

The Wedding

Fergus, straight away asked Manny for his daughter's hand in marriage, Manny looked at Madeleine for approval. She told her dad that she loved him very much. Manny already knew this by the look on her face. So her father said, "Yes" without further hesitation. Manny realised that he could not have asked for a better son in law.

The next day a great wedding was arranged in the village square, and everybody was invited. The marriage ceremony ended with these famous words, "I do", and "I now pronounce you man and wife". This was followed by rapturous applause from all the guests. After this there were lots of speeches arranged by the best man, Mac, Flea. His real name was Daniel. Daniel Mac Flea.

When all the appraisals, and congratulations were over, toasts were made to the bride and bridegroom. Teardrops found their way into the eyes of Mrs la Rue.

Daniel Mac Flea gave the nod for the music to begin, and the band struck up. The tunes were very lively, with loads of energetic dancing, jigging, and leaping all around the square. Then a beautiful heavenly choir started singing heart touching love songs. Great merrymaking was had by all in this tiny village. All the food was provided and prepared by Mrs La, Rue, aided by a multitude of willing helpers.

At last, Fergus had been tamed by the love of a good woman. This marital union eventually produced three sons, in fact they were triplets. They were called Markee, Twizzle, and Squitch. All were very handsome boys.

Fergus's life in the cauliflower was looking good. He became a very respected member of the community, and sat in on village council meetings. Fergus also arranged community games, organised fetes, and lots of important venues for the betterment of all the inhabitants. Perhaps, thought Fergus, one day they might make me Mayor of this lovely village.

CHAPTER 11

The Growth Of The Village

Now that Fergus's family was five in total, they needed somewhere to live. They knew that they could eat as much of the cauliflower as they wanted. There was no shortage of food, as the cauliflower was so large and they were so small. They could hollow out a whole room, and as time went by they even carved out small houses within the confines of the vegetable, with beds, chairs, and tables.

All kinds of furniture was carved out of the flesh of the cauliflower. The people in the village who had the biggest teeth got the largest jobs, such as house building, and road making, and the ones with the smallest teeth got the fine delicate work such as furniture making.

They even carved out a massive statue of Manny, as he was the founder of the community. They wanted to honour him for his leadership. The statue was erected in the village square, with a small unveiling ceremony. It became a meeting place in the village, locals would say, "See you at Mannys". Every body knew exactly where it was.

Nothing ever needed painting. Every item that was made, was already a lovely shade of ivory, as all cauliflowers are.

The tooth carvers made the village grow, and grow, by carving out boulevards and avenues. They also hewed out little bridges across flows of rain water which were regarded as rivers. Fergus hung a sign outside his front door which read, "Tickly Throat House" he was very proud of this name. Every thing was idyllic, and peaceful.

CHAPTER 12

A Family Squabble

The sons of Fergus were growing up very fast. They were now young adults with dreams of love. There were very few single females within the village. Where was one to find a future wife. The elders of the village realised this, and set up a small social club in the square. They now had a venue for Dances, and other social events to take place.

Markee, Squitch , and Twizzle were regular visitors. All three had no luck with the ladies, as there were more males than females. The girls had the pick of any boy they fancied.

CHAPTER 13

Emma

One evening Squitch was at the club on his own when his attention was drawn to what seemed like the perfect woman. She sat there all alone, looking ever so genteel. As he moved closer she looked straight into his eyes. His knees started knocking together. He could not even open his mouth to talk. She spoke first. "Hello, my name is Emma, what are you called". This put the ever so bashful Squitch at ease. He talked. She listened. His confidence was completely restored.

After loads of fun, lots of laughter, hand holding, and a little wooing, they realized that they had great deal in common. So Squitch asked Emma if she would like to meet his family. She agreed, and off they went towards the house of Fergus.

As they walked along, Squitch could not take his eyes off Emma. She was a stunner; dressed to kill, and adorned with the latest fashion. Fergus was in love. She was tall, slim, and had high cheekbones. She wore high heel shoes on all four of her feet. On her hands she wore black velvet gloves that stretched all the way up to the joints of her elbows. From the way she walked with a wonderful air of elegance, she looked the perfect model.

"Hi Mum this is Emma" said Squitch to his mother as she opened the door. Madeleine was charmed to meet such a beauty. "Come on in, you are most welcome". Emma entered the house, and verbally admired its structure, the walls, the high carved ceilings, and the furniture. Everything was so different to any other house she had seen before. It was so modern and comfortable. "I wish we had a house as good as this." said Emma.

Markee and Twizzle moved closer to Squitch's girlfriend. They were falling in love with Emma. All three brothers were spellbound. They started pushing and shoving each other for the attention of this unusual beauty in their midst. Emma realised there could be family trouble. She did not want to be responsible for this. There was no way that she could be the true girlfriend of all three brothers.

Emma was beginning to panic, she did not know what to do, so she quickly headed for the door, opened it, made a quick exit, and ran down the street. She completely disappeared into the night. Emma was never seen again by any of the family.

There was silence within the house. The triplets stared at each other in total disbelief. Tears began to flow in their eyes. The silence was awful, it continued for some time. They all had a feeling of emptiness.

The boys knew they would never see her again. Squitch was hurt the most, it took quite a long time to heal the pain in his heart. The loss of Emma was worse for him, but eventually he forgave his brothers for all the heartache that they had caused. Their friendship slowly returned to normal. However, Squitch never forgot the loss of Emma, this beautiful vision would be in his mind forever.

Fergus felt sorry for Squitch, after all he had just lost his very first girlfriend, but he felt even more sorry for his wife Madeleine. She had a twinkle in her eye, hoping for a grandchild or two. All she could do now was to look to the future, and hope.

However, the search for female company continued by the three boys. They would never give up.

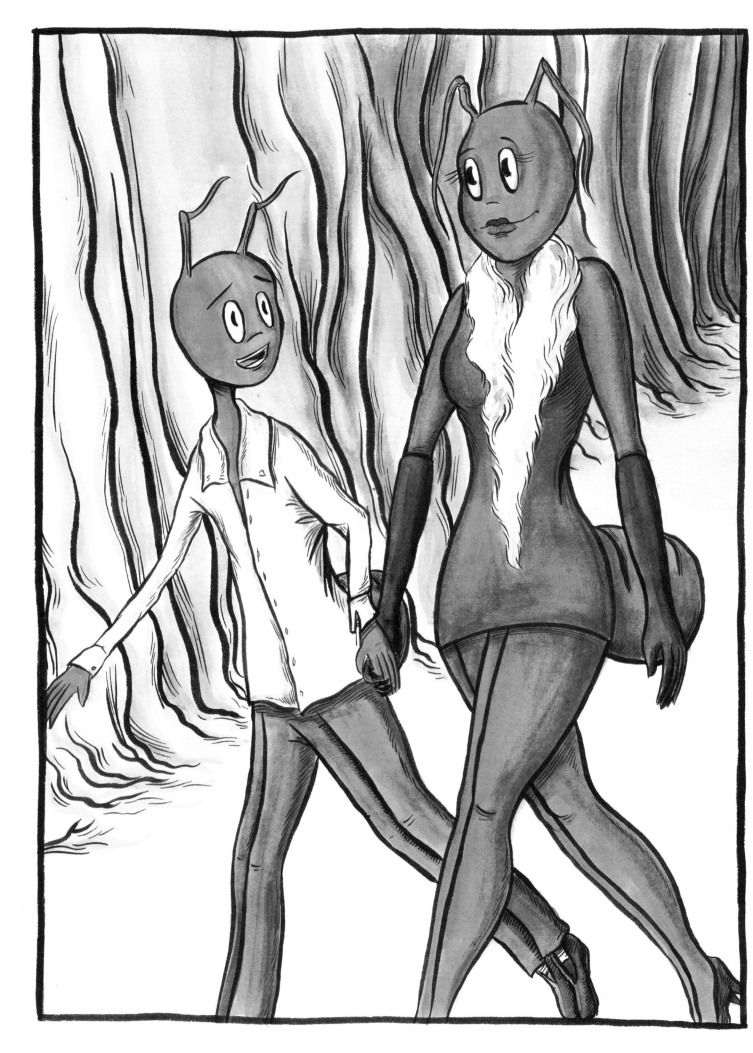

CHAPTER 14

The Dream

One day a thunderous voice boomed within the echoing caverns of the cauliflower. "Heed my warning" it said, "you must leave my body quickly. Soon I will be harvested, chopped up, cooked in boiling water and eventually eaten. Leave now if you want to save yourselves" Mr Fergus and his family were very frightened, they all ran out into the street, Mr Fergus, as he was now called, shouted, "But how can we escape and get out," his voice was very panicky. The loud response was. "Go to the centre of my body, there you will find a large crack in my root system. You must collect some of my green leaves to use as mats, and slide down the crack which leads to the outside world. This is your last warning", boomed the voice, "goodbye, goodbye". and the voice slowly faded away.

Manny, a seemingly wise old soul, who was listening to all this, said to Mr Fergus, "Take no heed, we have had lots of warnings, and nothing has happened so far". Mr Fergus felt reassured, and took his family back to Tickly Throat House. He thought no more about this awful warning. Life continued in happiness, and everything returned to normal.

Then Fergus woke up. He was sweating. It was all a horrible dream, "Thank god", said Fergus to himself. It would have broken his heart to have to leave such a lovely home as this.

CHAPTER 15

The Destruction Of The Village

One evening while they were all tucked up in bed, and fast asleep, they were rudely awakened by a loud chomping sound. Mr Fergus, was terrified. The bedroom shook as if a train was ploughing through it. The bed was tossed aside with him, and Maddy being thrown to the floor. He ran to his front door just in time to see it being sliced in two by what looked like larger than life teeth. It was a beast, in fact it was a cow. One of the largest animals they had ever seen. This bovine animal was eating the cauliflower for lunch. It had already swallowed half of it. All the roads, avenues, houses, and statues were disappearing before his very eyes. The floor of the family house was trembling beneath Fergus's feet. It felt as though it was just about to collapse. It was just like a strong earthquake.

Maddy threw a large bed sheet over her shoulders for protection and modesty. What was left of their home was just about to be eaten. The children and their mother were frozen with fear. Luckily Mr Fergus knew exactly what to do. He quickly gathered up his whole family in his arms and shouted, "Hang on tightly". He then jumped straight out into the unknown.

The whole family were still frantically clinging to each other for dear life, and screaming for help. They all managed to look back, and saw that the remains of the cauliflower had disappeared. They were terrified as they plummeted towards the earth, and certain death. But luck was on their side again. Mr Fergus noticed the large bed sheet over Maddy's shoulders and shouted, "Quick, each grab a corner of the bed cover". This they did, and they all floated gently to the ground, assisted by their makeshift parachute.

When they all had landed safely on the ground, Maddy quickly put the bed sheet back over her shoulders. Even with all the danger around, modesty was still a priority for her. Mr Fergus realised that they were now exposed to a new kind of danger. Predators, those that attack little creatures like him, and his lovely family, of which he was very proud. These predators would have them all for lunch, so he had to get them all to safety straight away.

They started running towards a small outcrop of rocks where they noticed that one boulder in particular had a tiny crack in it. Darkness was setting in rapidly, so they rushed quickly into the small opening, where they found refuge, and warmth. It was only now that they felt safe from the unknown.

CHAPTER 16

Winter

The animal had completely devoured their home, they were homeless. All of Maddy's family had gone, never to be seen again. She started crying, Mr Fergus and the children cuddled her. Only time would heal this sort of sorrow. The family were now all alone.

The cold grew worse. Winter was on its way, they could feel it in their bones. Life was growing more miserable day by day for the flea family. They foraged for what little food they could find, and to make things worse for them, light snow began to fall. It was time to hibernate, and save body energy. They all wrapped up together in the same quickly assembled bed. It was put together with bits of leaves and grass, and any other material they could find, this would keep them warm during their long slumber. Each one cuddled the other in order to retain maximum warmth, and they all went to sleep, for what was left of the winter. Nothing troubled them during their long sleep. They were totally worn out.

One morning they awoke to the sound of dripping water. The snow was melting, and it sounded great. The weather was warming up. It was a lovely feeling they got when they emerged from the safety of their home. The sun was shining, spring had arrived and food was plentiful. The boys went off exploring the surrounding area, and their mother started to prepare their tea. Things were looking good again.

CHAPTER 17

The Seed

One day the youngest of the family, Markee, called his dad to tell him he had found a large egg shaped item in the soil. Mr Fergus asked his son to take them to this mysterious object, and sure enough there it was lodged in the clay. It looked like something from outer space. They approached this unknown item with great caution. Fear was on their faces, but not on Maddy's. She was a very shrewd woman who was not easily fooled, she whipped out her homemade umbrella, and prodded it a few times. "Goodness me", exclaimed Maddy, "Its only a plant seed, and what's more I think its a giant seed from our old cauliflower home". Fergus quickly stepped forward, put his hand to his face, pondered for few seconds, and spoke. "What luck", said Mr Fergus, "we can cultivate this seed, and grow ourselves a completely new home". He went on to say, that there would be a fairly long waiting time before the seed would germinate. Even after that, they would have to wait a further amount of time until maturity took place.

But these were future worries, and the present problem was to work out a way of moving the seed nearer to the safety of their present home, get it planted, and support his family, all at the same time. This would be a mammoth task.

Nothing would put him off, Certain things must be done to protect the precious seed. Fergus thought it was so important to move it. Birds, and other kinds of animals do like to eat this kind of food. But how do you move a thing that size?.

One of the three kids, Squitch, said he had noticed a large box on the way here. It was packed with what looked like wooden stakes, there were loads of them scattered every where. In fact it was a lost box of matches that may have been dropped by some human. Mr Fergus went and inspected the box, and the items mentioned by Squitch. He found the wooden stakes were very light, and thought they could be moved and worked on. His plan was to construct some sort of cart to transport the seed. As Fergus was still rambling away to himself, Maddy stepped forward and said, "Don't be ridiculous, we are not super fleas, its just impossible to shift this seed, its much too heavy for us to move, just forget it". Fergus and the rest of the family agreed with Maddy.

They all felt very sad and low in spirit, the little group just sat there feeling very low, and out of ideas. "Is this the end, what are we going to do," said Mr Fergus. "Every thing has been against me. Sorry, I, meant us. I shall never give up. I have a loving wife, three wonderful boys, and we have survived all that has been thrown at us". He held his head in his hands, and felt despair. Tears crept into his eyes. A strange silence fell over the whole family.

CHAPTER 18

The Sadness

To comfort Fergus, Maddy, and the three children gathered around him. They all hugged and cried together. This was a very sad moment which went on for a long, long time. When the sadness and teardrops had all vanished, a calm feeling fell over the whole family. Nobody knew what to do next, a few minutes of silence prevailed.

This sad quiet period was suddenly broken by young Twizzle, who spoke. "I have a friend who could help".

Fergus looked at Twizzle, and said, "Who son, who could possibly come to our aid, what is this person called". Twizzle was a little hesitant, he thought his father would tell him off. "Come on son, who is it?". Twizzle now felt more at ease. "Well dad, his name is Willie; Willie the worm", replied Twizzle.

"I met him a while back in a field, not too far from our home. Willie was very friendly towards me. He is an extremely large creature. In fact, he probably is as big as a mountain. I might be exaggerating a little bit, but you just you wait until you see him, then you can judge for yourself ". Twizzle paused and drew his breath. "Anyway. Willie said to me if I ever wanted a favour, or help of any kind I should contact him. I have already told him all about our other problems, so he knows what kind of trouble we are in. He could move the seed and what's more, I bet he could even plant it for us".

Again there was more silence, they were all in deep thought. After a short time, Mr Fergus stood up and said," Well. Well, Well; this family cannot believe what we are hearing, a friendly worm. No, there is no such thing. We must be extra careful, he might see us as food and eat us". But Mr Fergus did not have very much choice, he just had to trust his favourite son's judgement.

After a lot more debating, and arguing with the whole family, Mr Fergus sat back down, and held both his hands out to motion his family to be quiet. He then turned to Twizzle. "It seems that we are all in agreement to get in touch with this large worm character, but how do we contact Willie, where can we find him. I am sure its going to be very difficult. As you know, all worms live far below the soil, we certainly are unable to burrow down into the soil to find him."

Young Twizzle stood up, looked at his father, and said "Well Dad, Willie once told me, that if ever I wanted his help, all I would have to do is to signal him by tapping three times on the rock outside our cave. I would have to use the largest pebble that I could possibly lift, and he would come to our aid. Apparently this tapping noise travels through the ground to his very sensitive ears, and no matter where he is, or what he is doing, he will hear the signal, and come to investigate."

Fergus was quick to speak, "It all sounds good to me son, but, before we return home, we must hide our priceless seed. Some bird or slug might find it, and treat it as a meal. They all agreed, and the seed was duly hidden by various bits of vegetation that they found lying around the area.

When the task was completed, and the group were happy with the camouflage, they were eager to start the homeward journey. Fergus said, "Let's go," and in a flash, our little heroes were off down the track with great haste. They wanted to get on with this tapping business as soon as possible. The family had nothing to lose, and everything to gain.

Fergus and his tiny band quickly made their way back to their rocky crevice home, and as they had been out all day, they needed a little sustenance, such as a drink of water. When they were well fed and watered, they gathered around the particular rock mentioned by Twizzle. There was an eerie silence, they were extremely excited, especially the triplets. Twizzle stood there holding the biggest pebble he thought he could lift high above his head.

The tension was unbearable. Twizzle looked at each member of the family in turn. "Come on Twizzle", said Squitch, "get on with it". Twizzle had trouble lifting the pebble.' Markee stepped forward to assist him. They both raised it together with ease. Then the pebble was brought crashing down once, twice, and, then a third time on the half buried rock at the entrance to their cave.

CHAPTER 19

Willie The Worm

Nothing happened for quite a while. The silence was unbearable. Suddenly, a very loud noise began behind them. The ground trembled, and seemed to shake as if Doomsday had arrived.

Something was going on behind them. They all turned their heads. The family were all very frightened, they did not know what was about to happen. The soft earth was moving, it was like an earthquake, with soil was rising up like a volcano, bringing with it, small pebbles. These pebbles then started to roll down the side of the ever growing mountain of earth. The pebbles looked like giant boulders to the tiny flea family. Squitch shouted, "Get back, everybody get back, we are all in danger". They need not have worried, as it was all over as quickly as it had started.

The movement of the earth had stopped, and there at the top of the earth mound, was this gigantic creature known as Willie the Worm, in all his glory. He looked enormous. He was like the Pirelli tyre man. He looked like a gigantic stack of lorry tyres, with a smiling head, and big laughing eyes, his colour was like that of a glowing candle, radiating warmth.

Willie was swaying to and fro, like a lofty American Indian totem pole. He looked like a jolly giant, and looked as if he could be trusted. The flea family no longer felt scared, they just stared upwards in total awe.

"Hello Twizzle", said Willie, "do you need my help. I did promise you the earth and I did not mean soil". Willie laughed at his own little joke. It sounded like thunder. "I am sorry if I frightened you by all that earth movement. I do hope you are all ok. I know you called me here for some sort of assistance, so just say what help you require, and I will do what I can. I must say that you Twizzle are one of my very few, and lovable little friends, but who are the others".

Willie could not believe the fear he had caused to this small shocked group. In future he would have to take much more care when he made an exit from the ground.

Twizzle stepped forward and said, "This is my Dad, my Mom, and these are my two brothers, Markee and Squitch". Willie swayed a little in the breeze. "Lovely to meet you", he said. Willie had one eye on the flea family, and the other scanning the sky. He was checking for predators from above. His worst enemy were birds, and birds knew that Willie would make a very tasty lunch.

Willie would have to be extra careful, after all, he was extremely exposed above the soil. He would easily be spotted from high in the sky by these sharp eyed feathered creatures. They were so fast, and he had absolutely no protection.

My Dad will explain our problem", said Twizzle. "Even though I have told you most of it, I would prefer him to tell to you everything".
Mr Fergus stepped forward, placed his thumbs in his waistcoat pockets, and looking like the dickens character called Mr Bumble. He looked up, and began to speak.

"Well", said Mr Fergus, "I am delighted to meet you at last, I do hope you can help us, you see, the problem is this". Mr Fergus hesitated for a little breath, and went on to speak.

"We have spent the most enjoyable part of our existence living inside a vegetable. We had a lovely home in a wonderful idyllic village, with lots of families, and friends. This village was actually within the confines of a giant cauliflower. We thought nothing would ever go wrong.

But things did go wrong. Everything was destroyed by a large animal, actually it was a very hungry cow, and it just ate everything. We were very lucky to escape with our lives. The cow did not know the damage it would do to our whole community, but she has to eat just like every other living being, and so we were all made homeless. It's our dream to create another village similar to the one we lost".

"Fortunately", said Fergus, "I and my lovely family were spared by some higher being". Fergus drew another couple of large breaths, he then continued. "We were lucky to have found a cauliflower seed, which we would like to plant, and cultivate into another giant cauliflower, but it's too big for us to move and plant, so it's to you that we have turned to."

Fergus continued speaking. "What we would like you to do is move the seed near to our present home, where the soil is very fertile, dig a hole, plant the seed, and cover it with soil. Then all we have to do is wait until it grows into a mature cauliflower. You see, we aim to construct a completely new village within this vegetable. I know it's a bit ambitious, but we must give it a try. So we turn to you for help, the ball is now in your court". Mr Fergus stepped back to be near his family.

Willie smiled, at least he now knew he had a chance to repay them for the fear he had put them through. "No problem", roared Willie. "Take me to the place where this seed is, so that I can make a plan, and get started. It sounds like a very simple task to me." said Willie. There was a strange quietness for a while; they all hoped Willie knew what he was doing.

Fergus stood up, and spoke again, he told Willie that it would take quite a while to walk to the place where the seed was. He also told him that, they being so small, and he is so large, maybe he could give them a lift.
"What a great idea," said Willie "In that case I better lower my torso and you can jump up on my back". Willie bent over, and said, "come on then, up you get, I don't move very fast, but I'm fifty times faster than you, and don't forget, hold on for dear life". Willie bent down near the ground, and everybody hopped on. They were all feeling very excited now.

"Point the way", said Willie, and off they went like the Hammers of Hell. What a ride they all had!. They were already looking forward to the return journey, even thought they had not yet completed the exciting outward trip.

After a short time Fergus shouted "Here we are", Willie slowed down and then came to a full stop next to the hidden seed. The flea family were still so excited after the breathtaking ride that they could not even speak for a while. Willie had to wait until they had all calmed down in order to speak to them.

When they had recovered enough from all the excitement, they showed Willie where the seed was hidden. "So this is the item you want me to plant for you," Willie nudged and prodded it with his snout like nose, he rolled it over a few times to check its quality and when he was satisfied, he said. "I can see no problem with this task, I just wish there was something I could transport it in". Fergus told him about the discarded match box down the path, he said the inner tray could be used to move the precious seed in.

Willie said "What a great idea" and was gone in a flash shooting down the path like a bullet. Things went quiet when Willie was gone, the family felt very lonely at this point. They already missed Willie, even though he had just left.

After a short time a loud noise emerged from down the pathway. It was Willie returning, pushing the tray with such strength, and speed that Fergus could not believe it. Willie did impress everybody, they had never met such a gentle and powerful giant. They always thought that worms were sluggish, and useless, but not this one. He was their hero, and they just loved him for what he was. "Right", said Willie, "I must get on with it. "Stand well back; I need plenty of room".

Willie leaned over the seed, wiggled his lips a few times, and produced some sort of a sticky goo from his mouth. He covered the seed in this gluey like substance. He then picked up the seed, and popped it into the matchbox tray. The seed was now stuck fast to the floor of the tray, and ready for transporting. All the flea family just looked on in amazement; this was something completely new to them.

CHAPTER 20

A Worm With Arms

When the job was all done, Willie, said, "Ok,   hop in and we'll be off". Willie was so eager to get going that they just about managed to leap into the matchbox tray. Willie started to push the seed container back towards the family home with great speed. They were all thrown to the back of the matchbox tray. The noise was unbelievable. There was nothing to hold on to except each other. They all bounced around like marbles, it was all a bit scary. The noise was deafening.

When they were half way through their homeward journey, the on board family were getting thrown about even more. Willie was still pushing the tray just like a demon. He seemed not to tire. They were trudging along, with not far to go, when the unexpected happened.

Willie was shoving with all his strength, making the matchbox tray plough through soil and grass. It suddenly hit a semi submerged rock, and came to an abrupt halt. This sudden stop, caught all of the flea family by surprise, causing all of them to shoot straight out of the tray, and upwards towards the sky. The seed stayed exactly where it was, it, of course being stuck fast by Willie's goo.

All the family were waving their little arms and legs franticly, they were all flying without power, Willie heard their pleas for help, and he would not ignore them. He knew that something would have to be done with great haste. He straightened up his body, so he was at the same level as the screaming flying fleas. He had to act very quickly, or his little friends could all be very badly injured. To make things worse, they had reversed their ascent, and were now beginning to plummet towards the ground.

It was unbelievable what Willie did next. He produced hidden hands and arms from under the rolls, and folds of his skin.

This was a great surprise to Mr Fergus and family, as they thought worms did not have arms, or hands. Furthermore, nobody had ever seen a worm with such limbs. They were even more flabbergasted, when to their great delight when Willie put these hidden limbs to use. He grabbed each of the family one by one, before they hit the ground. He used amazing speed to carry out this action.

One, by one, he put them gently back into the safety of the matchbox tray. Willie said, "Sorry about that folks, I did not expect any thing like that to happen". He then moved the tray around the submerged rock. They were off once again at breath taking speed. The noise was even louder now, the family were even more scared. They just wished this journey would end now.

When they arrived back at their home the noise had stopped. The five little passengers all jumped out very quickly. They were glad to be back on the ground again. Some of them felt a little queasy, but at least they had the seed exactly where they wanted it. All they wanted now was a drink, just to calm down. They had to relax for a while in order to get over their amazing journey.

Soon they all recovered sufficiently from their ordeal to show Willie where they wanted the seed planted. It was easy for Willie to dig a hole in the soil, after all. He does live in the soil, and it's a natural thing for a worm to do. Willie quickly dug the hole with his great big snout, planted the seed with a bit of his special goo to moisten and fertilize it. He then covered it with soil, and padded the area down with his rear end. Willie then overturned the match box tray, and pushed it over the planted seed, then he sealed it up with more goo from his mouth.

"There you are, all done," said Willie. "The seal will stop the damp getting in, and prevent the seed from rotting. Soon the rains will be here to give life to the seed, and I bet you will be pleased with the results when germination takes place.

Willie leaned down towards his lovable little friends and said, "I have to go now, I must return to my world, and my other friends. I have only been gone a short time, and I miss them all very much.

We are off on a bit of a holiday soon. Its in an apple orchard, we get one apple each, and as it's self-catering, you just help yourself, it might be a bit boring", Willie laughed at his little joke, "We know the farmer wont like it, but that's life. I can't wait to get there, so Goodbye, my little pals, Goodbye".

Maddy wanted him to stay for tea, but she would have had to cook for a week to feed him, what with Willie being so enormous, so she said goodbye to him like the rest of the family.

Willie bent over, and smiled, he winked at each of the family in turn, as a goodbye gesture. It seemed to take a long time for his eye lid to close, and reopen. Each wink was done with great affection.

When all the farewells were over, and done, Willie nose dived into the soil and vanished, leaving a hollow crater, with small pebbles rolling down the inside, and the outside of the mound that he had just created. They still had to jump out of the way of these pebbles for fear of injury.

Willie had returned to the soil from where he had emerged. He was gone. The whole visit was awesome, they would never forget him. They would miss him a great deal, his sheer power, his size, his friendly smile, where would anyone find a worm with arms. It's a good thing that he did have these hidden limbs; otherwise they would all be dead.

They could not say enough in his favour. Everything about him was a fantasy; he would be in their minds forever. When he was gone, the silence was noticeable. They returned to their temporary dwelling, and talked about Willie until they all fell fast asleep.

CHAPTER 21

The Germination

The end of spring was approaching very quickly, the weather was much warmer. The sun was peeping through the trees, birds were singing, and life was getting easier. So far they had no problems what so ever.

One morning they heard a loud snapping noise that came from just outside their abode. They were all startled, and wondered what it was. The whole group speedily ran outside with great apprehension on their faces, but they need not have worried. Under the matchbox tray something was happening. The seed was germinating. Its outer case had cracked open, just like the shell of an egg. The roots shot downwards into the soil, looking for moisture. The matchbox tray was thrown aside by the sheer power of the growing seed. This was the pure strength of Mother Nature at its best, and nothing on earth could stop it.

"Thank God", said Mr Fergus. His eyes were glazed with tears of happiness as he watched the young plant grow upwards towards the sky, this dynamic, and speedy growth was attributed to Willies extra strength goo. It had acted as a powerful fertiliser, feeding the plant with lots of extra rich nutrients. This is what plants thrive on, nourishment.

The family all held hands and formed a circle, they then performed a little dance of joy. Songs of thanksgiving were sung. The group were so happy that they could not stop dancing until they were all worn out. They were so tired that they just lay down, and fell fast asleep on the spot. They slept late into the afternoon of the next day.

Daily, they watched the stalk of the baby cauliflower grow, with leaves forming on its green stalk as it headed upwards towards the heavens. From now on, Mr Fergus thought, all was going to be good, he could now relax. A big smile crept all over his face.

They watched the cauliflower grow and grow until the top disappeared out of their sight. To these tiny insects it looked like one of the New York skyscraper buildings they had heard of. It would take a very long time for the head and florets of the vegetable to develop fully, so they would have to check on its growth every day. They were wondering how they could possibly reach the top. Not only that, they also had to gain access to the inner core of the cauliflower.

There were lots of problems ahead, but they would worry about that when the time was right. All they could do was wait.

CHAPTER 22

The Purple People

One day, the whole family were sitting chatting about all the exciting things that had happened to them in days gone by, items that had affected their lives, and more so, the loss of Maddies family. This little get together made them all stronger. A much more united family emerged.

Squitch, Markee and Twizzle were much older now, and just like young adults, they longed for female company of their own age. There were none, maybe, they thought, one day this might all change.

One evening, just after they had had their supper, the group were startled by noises. It sounded like voices coming from the nearby bramble bush. This made them frightened, as they thought they were completely alone. They were worried by these sounds so they crouched down to hide. Brave Mr Fergus timidly shouted, "Who's there, Show yourself".

After a long moment of silence a voice said, "Don't be alarmed, we're coming out". Mr Fergus and family could not believe their eyes, as all these dark shadows appeared. One materialised into Manny, Maddy's father, and standing behind him were most of the villagers from the old destroyed cauliflower. Maddy was overcome with emotion. She had thought her ninety nine brothers and sisters were all dead. There was her mother, her father, and all the other friends she thought she had lost.

This was a most unexpected reunion. They hugged and cried with joy, Fergus thought a miracle had just happened.

After all the excitement had died down Mr Fergus noticed something odd about all his old friends. They were all purple. "What happened", asked Mr Fergus. "Why are all of you purple". Manny replied, "Well it's like this, when our cauliflower was bitten in half by a very large animal. I think it was called a cow that was only having its lunch. We can not honestly blame the beast".

Manny continued. "As the cow took her first bite, we all went hurtling towards the ground, and certain death. But thanks to the Almighty, we were very lucky to be scooped up by a stray cauliflower leaf that had fallen from the cow's mouth. We all hung on tight to this God sent leaf. We then floated gently downwards, and landed on top of a blackberry bush. Then we helped each other to climb down these very thorny bramble branches to the safely of the ground".

Manny continued, "The soil was covered with ripe blackberries, they were everywhere, and that was all we had to eat. So this is why we are all purple. Its from the dye in the juice giving us this strange colour. It will wear off in time, but never mind all that". Manny reached out his arms towards Maddy. "Come and give your old Dad another big hug Maddy". She embraced her father very tightly, and there was a great deal of joy within the small crowd.

Mr, Fergus told all his old friends everything about the cauliflower seed, and how it had developed into a very large vegetable. He also told them that the ivory ball was surrounded by a nest of green leaves. It would not be long before it was fully developed.

Fergus took all of them to the spot where the vegetable was growing.
They were amazed at what they saw. All these little insects gathered around the stalk of the cauliflower, and started to walk around the base of their expected new home. It was great exercise for all.

They called it the Cauliflower Walk. It was used morning, noon, and night. They also used it for lots of social gatherings, where they were able to meet, walk and talk.

During one of these many social assemblies, Mr Fergus told them all about Willie the worm. His great name, for instance rang in their heads. It was just pure fairy tale material, and also it was his huge size that caused most excitement among the little band of survivors. The demands on poor old Fergus for more, and more stories about Willie was beginning to wear him out.

CHAPTER 23

A Celebration Ball

The next day a great, and joyous ball was arranged in a clearing nearby. This was to celebrate the reunification of all the village people. The old matchbox tray was quickly found, and pushed into place by the young and strong of the group. They overturned it and then decorated it as a band stand for all the musicians to sit on.

When the band were ready to play, they simply rubbed their arms together just as a cricket rubs his back legs. The sound was similar to lots of violins playing lively jiggy music.

Manny, and his wife led the dance, closely followed by Fergus, and Madelaine. Next came all the other happy dancers, they were promenading, doze doeing, and generally yelling with high spirits all around the clearing. Markee, Twizzle, and Squitch all had found partners. It was obvious to their parents that their children were slowly falling in love. The merry making went on until dawn, and by this time they were all worn out. But what a great time they had.

CHAPTER 24

Out Of Reach

The day arrived when the cauliflower was fully grown and ready for use. All the village survivors were straining their necks by looking skywards. They could see the cauliflower had now swollen to an enormous size, with large green leaves cradling the closely knitted ivory florets of this super sized vegetable. It was gigantic to these small insects. They were dwarfed by the sheer size of the plant, it swayed to and fro in the gentle breeze like a giant redwood tree.

"Oh my goodness" said Manny "How on earth are we going to reach the top, and gain entry". Nobody had a clue what to do, it was time for much brain work but not a single idea was produced from the whole crowd. No one could think of any way to reach these lofty heights. One hour had passed, and a lot of useless ideas were put forward by various adults. Deadlock was reached, everybody went silent, and nobody had any more to say. They all wondered what they could possibly do now.

Two of the sons of Fergus stood up, Markee, and Squitch had been whispering together, and when they had risen, they jointly made a brilliant suggestion. "Why don't we send for Willie the Worm once more, he helped us last time, and were sure he will help us again"? All the newcomers wanted to meet this legendary worm, and so they did not need very much persuading. After a little more discussion, they all agreed.

CHAPTER 25

The Return Of Willie The Worm

Twizzle, and Markee were put in charge of getting in contact with Willie. So the giant worm was duly summoned by tapping on the main rock three times outside their home, just as they did before.

The entire crowd were waiting for Willie to appear. They were nervous. Everybody looked very scared, and anxious. They knew what had happened previously, with the moving earth, and lots of dangerous pebbles rolling about.

Last time Mr Fergus and family had to run for their lives, but this time they did not have to worry. Willie knew he would have to be very careful when he finally emerged from the soil, he knew the extent of the injuries he could cause to these tender little creatures. It could be awful, and may even be fatal.

This time Willie slowly rose out of the ground with very little earth movement. There he stood again, like some sort of a giant God, his torso seemed to be even larger this time. Willie was again scanning the sky with one eye, and looking towards the crowd with the other. "My little friends, it's lovely to see you again", he said with his deep echoing voice.

This great worm towered above them. "You seem to have increased your family by quite a lot, they all look so friendly, but enough of that, how can I help you". He bent over in half, bringing his great head down near the ground, so that he was able to look them square in the eye. This time Manny took the chair, after all he was the head of the group. He told Willie all the new problems they were having. The big worm listened very intently to Manny.

Willie thought for quite a while, then he looked up at the tall cauliflower, and studied it for some time. It was then that he realised that it was at least thirty times taller than he was. He returned his gaze to Manny and Fergus, and said; "I am afraid there is nothing I can do to help. There is no way I could carry all of you to such a great height, some of you might fall and get badly hurt. Even if I did reach the top I would probably get dizzy, and crash back to the ground resulting in severe injuries to all of us. I just could not risk such a perilous assent. You will have to forget about help from me, it's totally out of the question," said the giant worm. Everybody looked stunned. Silence prevailed.

CHAPTER 21

Willie The Nurse

Willie broke the silence, "Hang on, I have just thought of a friend who might be able to help. It's a long time since I have seen her. She owes me a very big favour."

Willie continued to talk, "She is a very large and beautiful butterfly called Laurali, who is apparently, named after the Queen of the fairies. I am not too sure about the fairy tale name. I know she has no connection with Fairies whatsoever, anyway, that is beside the point. Let me get on with the story. She crash landed once, not too far away from my home. She had been attacked by a marauding nasty multicoloured wasp. He had terrorised her in flight, He then immobilised her with a light sting to the body, causing a great deal of pain. This caused her to crash, resulting in the breaking of two of her many legs, there was also damage to one of her wings. She was helpless when I found her."

Willie went on to say, "Laurali was in mortal danger of being eaten alive by all sorts of predators, such as birds, voles, frogs, or any other carnivorous thing that happened to pass by. I quickly covered her with bits of leaves, grass, and anything else that I could find.

When I knew she was well and truly hidden from these predatory creatures, I made splints from various bits of twigs. Then I used some of my special goo to bind these odd bits to her broken legs and wing. Her fractures set very quickly. It must have been my amazing healing goo that done the trick. She was as right as rain in a couple of weeks."

Willie continued, "As Laurali flew off, she shouted "I am in your debt Willie, anything you want, any favour, you just name it, I will be there. I owe you much Willie". She then disappeared above the trees. I have not seen her since that accident, but I do know where she is, and It will be very easy for me to contact her". Willie paused for a breath, and then went on to say, "I am sure she will assist in any way, all I have to do is ask."

The big worm now had a tear in his eye as he addressed the tiny assembly. "Laureli will be able to fly all of you to the top of the cauliflower, she is much bigger and stronger than me." Willie had   another pause, and then continued to speak. "You know, I would have made a great nurse, I think I missed my vocation in life".

Willie went on to say, "I am getting hungry now, so I must leave soon, there is no way you could supply me with the vast quantities of food that I require".

The village people were all spell bound by Willie's confidence, they were left staring up at him for quite some time. The giant worm paused for a while, and went into deep thought. After a short period of time he continued to speak. " This is what I would like you all to do after I have gone. You must help Laurali to land as near as possible to where you all now live, so if you could mark out a clearing nearby."

Willie pointed to a flat area close by, "What about over there, it looks like a good spot for her to drop in. It would assist Laurali if you could mark out a clear runway. Use anything you can find to guide her in, I am sure you know what I mean".

It was nearly time for Willie to go, he pulled himself up to his maximum height, and to the amazement of the crowd, produced his many arms, and hands. Willie then stretched these limbs outwards, and followed by a long large yawn. This stretching made him tower so high that the little people could hardly see his head. It was so far away. He then bent back down towards his tiny friends.

He scanned each of them with his big watery tearful eyes, and said, "I will go to my butterfly friend now, and explain everything to her, I have no doubt that she will help, so expect her in two days time. It will be late in the afternoon."

Before Willie left, he told them that he was going on another of his little holiday trips. "Last time" he said, "We went to an apple orchard, but this time it will be held in a pear orchard, and I must find myself a partner, so we will be eligible as a pair." Willie laughed at his double meaning joke, he then said, "I must be off now, so please stand well back. It was lovely to see you all again. I wish you all well, and good luck with Laurali, She will take very good care of all of you."

Willie slowly sank beneath the soft earth, he was very mindful not to hurt any of his little friends. He disappeared beneath the soil with such grace, and very little effort. Just a few pebbles rolled harmlessly back inside the crater. He left a lot of little insects gaping into the big hole that he had just opened, silence prevailed within the tiny group.

Willie had vanished. They all looked at each other, with tears in their eyes. Sadly, and slowly they unwillingly disbanded. The giant worm was gone forever, they would never see their idol again. Some were still crying the next day.

All they talked about for the next two days was Willie the giant worm, and all his amazing feats.

CHAPTER 21

The Anxious Wait

Laurali was due to land in two days time. These two days dragged on and on. It seemed more like two weeks. All the little insects could talk about was Willie this, and Willie that. They also talked of the forthcoming arrival of Laurali. They just could not wait.

Would she be friendly?. Would she be big, and beautiful as they were told?. Will she be as colourful as they were expecting. All these questions would soon to be answered. The whole group had great expectations. Who could blame them.

CHAPTER 28

A Nest Of Fireflies

Fergus and Manny were having a bit of a chat, Manny said "I have been thinking about the arrival of Laurali. She is due to arrive on a late afternoon, it may be a little dark. Willie told us to mark out a landing strip, so I thought about the nest of Fireflies in the next field, we could ask them to light up the runway, and make it easy for her to land". "What a great idea", said Fergus.

A small delegation of villagers went to talk to these tiny winged insects. They found the Fireflies were extremely friendly, and seemed very eager to help. It may be too dark on the arrival day, and the lighting from the Fireflies would be ideal. These small Flies radiated natural light from the top of their bodies. The amount of light from one insect was dim, but with so many Flies, it was thought the end effect would be bright enough.

A squadron was formed for the occasions. It was called the Flying Furry Fire Flies, or the Four F squadron for short. The runway was already marked out with bits of this, and bits of that. A practice run was arranged. The Four Fs took off en masse. They were like a squadron of dive bombers. There were hundreds of them. They headed straight for the runway, and dived down to their designated positions. They then activated their body lights and waited five minutes. When their leader, Captain Luke Flywalker was satisfied, they all took off, and vanished into thin air.

CHAPTER 29

Laurali The Butterfly.

As expected, on the second day, the whole crowd had assembled near the outer fence of the makeshift runway. These fences were constructed by friendly spiders spinning their web materials to mark out both sides of the landing strip. Every local insect wanted to help the villagers. The Fireflies, and the spiders all worked together.

The whole community was ready to travel, and had gathered all their belongings together for the trip. They were looking up towards the sky expecting to get a glimpse of Laurali. It was slightly dark. The moon was slowly rising, and casting long dark shadows everywhere.

Soon the waiting would be over. All the tiny fireflies were lined up on either side of the runway. Their twinkling lights were on full power. They were ready to guide Laurali to the pick up spot.

"There", shouted Markee, as he pointed towards the sky. Sure enough Willie had kept his word. The crowd surged forward. There she was, unmistakably approaching the ground. Slowly, but surely, a large dark shadow began to loom at the end of the runway. This shadow was getting larger and larger, and gradually. They were able to see that it was taking the shape of a very large wide winged butterfly. "It's her", they all cried out.

As the image was now very near the ground, they could plainly see by the light of the moon that it was Laurali, gliding in silently, on a warm current of air. She was slowly decreasing her height as she approached the landing strip. Her long legs ploughed up a little soil as she came to a perfect halt.

Her wingspan seemed to go on for ever. Her eyes were brown, they were extra large for a butterfly. She had extremely long eye lashes, they were moving up and down all the time, just like Spanish hand held dancing fans. Her body was of many bright colours, mainly crimson and yellow, with little splashes of green at the tail end of her torso. She was a sight to behold. Her long slender legs were slightly bent at the knee. These long legs made her tower above all the villagers.

Laurali ploughed up a little more soil as she bent her many legs, in order to nestle her long body into a good parking position. Her head turned left and right to look at those who had assembled there to greet her. There seemed to be a permanent smile on her face. This was the legend known as Laurali, and all loved what they saw.

They could just about see the wing tips of this stunning creature. It was because the ends of these flying limbs were so far away from the middle of her body. She was gigantic, just like a Zeppelin, with two wings on either side of her torso. Her legs were very. very long. with knee joints three quarters along each leg. She was so slender.

Soon the villagers apprehension of the unknown disappeared, they were not afraid anymore. Everybody ran towards her just to be near this apparition. They just wanted to admire her beauty.

Eventually, in a gentle velvety voice, she said, "Who speaks for you" It was more like a purring sound than a voice. "I do", said Manny as he eagerly stepped forward. "You are most welcome in our tiny community, we need your help very badly. Our mutual friend Willie the Worm spoke very highly of you, he said you might be able to assist us with our problem".

Manny went on to explain the catastrophe of their lost home, and how the new vegetable was now mature enough to be occupied, but they could not reach the top in order to gain entry. He told her what Willie the Worm had said. The big worm thought she would be able to fly the whole group to the top of the cauliflower.

There was silence for a time then, Laurali spoke. "Of course I can help. I saw the large object in question, as I glided in to the landing area,

CHAPTER 30

The Big Snooze

Laurali went on to say. "I am afraid it's a little too late to attempt the flight as its getting too dark". She lowered her head and said. "Anyway; I need a good nights sleep, I am worn out after my long flight here, and need to recuperate". She asked them all to stand back a little, as she was just about to change the position of her body. She did not want to cause any accidental injury to these little people.

Her vast pairs of wings slowly, and gracefully folded. Her long gangly legs bent at the knees to allow her body to drop even more to the ground. She then gently nestled her underbelly deeper into the soft soil, and when she was comfortable, Laurali said "Wake me at dawn". She then dropped her long eye lashes to close her eyes. She went straight to sleep, in order to rest before the big task ahead of her.

During the rest period, Laurali purred all the time that she slept.

At the crack of dawn Laurali had not opened her eyes, The crowd were all getting anxious. Squitch was getting impatient. He moved closer, and was just about to prod her torso with a long stick.

Laurali suddenly came to life, her body jerked a few times. It was then that she slowly opened her big brown eyes, stretched her long legs, fanned her wings, and said "I am ready now if you are." All the village people rushed forward, as if to stampede. This could have been dangerous, and would cause injury to the youngest of the group.

Manny soon realised this, he rushed forward with great haste, raised both his hands, and shook them vigorously at the crowd. "Stop" he roared " We must have order", he then raised his voice a bit more.

"Please". He paused for the reaction, and then he roared again. "Stop now". This last roar did the trick, they all stopped straight away, taking great care of the minors in their midst. They did not want to injure any of the younger members of the group with this abrupt halt. This panic was only caused by the excessive excitement of the forthcoming journey.

Due to the authority of Manny, the threatened stampede was over. They looked up to him, and treated him as their father figure. He was always shown great respect. Order soon prevailed. They all lined up to await their turn.

Laurali gracefully unfolded her wings, and stretched them fully outwards. She then lowered the tips to the ground and said, "Walk up both sides to the centre of my body where you will find a large groove on my back. You can all sit down and hold on to the fine hairs growing there, It will be a gentle ride, so don't worry, you will all be safe".

Manny ordered a mass exodus, and they all trudged along her wings, all the way to the top of her body, as instructed. It was a sight to behold, to actually see four lines of very excited insects, all marching up the wings of Laurali.

When they reached the top, they all nestled down together, in the hollow of her back. They then held on very tight. They felt that they were in an aeroplane with no cockpit cover.

When all were settled in the small of Laurali's back, she said, "Hold tight everybody, I hope you are all ready". There was a great chorus of "Ok", and "lets go" echoing from her rear.

Then Fergus shouted in panic. "Wait, where is Maddy, she's missing", Fergus, and Manny asked Laurali to wait a while. She agreed, and they both ran down to the ground, and after looking, and calling, all around Laurali, they did not find her. So they raced towards their old rock house.

They entered the dwelling and found Maddy crying on the bed. "What's wrong my love, don't you want to go?." Said Fergus. She threw her arms around him, and through the tears, she explained her sorrow at having to leave a place that she had grown to love so much. Manny and Fergus just about managed to persuade her to leave, by telling her the benefits of their future life. Eventually she agreed to go.

The pain on the faces of Manny, and Fergus changed to happiness. All three quickly returned to Laurali. They raced up her wing, and made themselves ready for take off. All three were completely breathless.

CHAPTER 31

The Doomed Flight

Laurali very slowly straightened out her knees, in order to give her elevation. She then raised her great wing tips from the ground, flapped them gently. Her body floated gently off the ground. Very soon she was airborne, she started heading upwards towards the top of the cauliflower.

All the little insects could see, was the ground disappearing from their view, they could not even see their old rock dwelling. Now they were really frightened, and all they could do was, hang on for dear life.

Laurali circled around, and around the top of the cauliflower hoping to find a suitable spot to settle. There was nothing. One more try, she thought, so she went around again, and managed to settle on a large ivory floret of the cauliflower. Laurali thought all was well now, but she was wrong. She started to slip, she was unable to hold on any longer. Laurali let go, again she was airborne. She still wanted to try again, but she was getting a bit tired now.

Things had gone badly wrong. There was no way she could maintain elevation. She just had to lighten the load. The flight was now unsafe. Laurali had to set her large cargo down straight away. She was having difficulty maintaining altitude due to all of these little passengers. One was very light, but there were so many of them. They all added up to an overload.

Laurali had misjudged their weight, they were dragging her down. She was now beginning to panic, and this forced her to totally abandon the landing on the cauliflower.

Fergus and Manny realised, to their horror that, any more attempts at landing were off. Laurali was heading towards a thick clump of bushes. She was sure that there was nothing else to do, but to unload as quickly as possible, or crash.

Panic broke out amongst the passengers. Manny tried to restore calm. Laurali was now circling a group of thyme bushes. She hovered over one particular bush, and shouted. "Quick, jump". The whole group abandoned Laurali with great haste. All had landed without injury.

CHAPTER 32

The Complete Circle

Laurali had dropped the whole cargo on one particular thyme bush. It looked very familiar to Fergus. As it turned out, it was the same thyme bush that Mr Fergus was born on. Such a coincidence was unbelievable, and he could not believe it. Soon all the little insects came together to regroup. They had to await instructions from their leader. Manny.

When Laurali was sure the last passenger was off, she said, "I am terribly sorry to let you all down like this". She felt a little ashamed, but nobody had the heart to blame her. Once again, she said "Sorry my little friends, I am so sorry." Even this apology was said with such a lovely feeling that soon little tear drops began to appear in everybody's eyes.

Then she flew away with sadness in her big beautiful brown eyes, and that was the last they ever saw of her. What a memory she left in all of their minds. They would have great stories to tell their future children, even though the attempt to land on the cauliflower was a total failure.

They had been abandoned on a thyme bush leaf that was known to Fergus. This was good, thought Mr Fergus, as he knew animals passed regularly beneath such bushes. All they had to do was wait, and sure enough, along trotted a very large dog.

CHAPTER 33

At Last A Proper Home

The tension was awful as they waited for the order. "Wait, not yet; Wait". Shouted Manny. And then the order came. "Jump", and they all leapt together. They did not have far to fall as the dogs back was just almost touching the thyme leaf. The whole group landed safely on the dog, where all fleas belong. They spread out in every direction. Their intention was to completely colonise this unfortunate dog.

What an adventure Fergus had been on. As he looked around, he saw what looked like familiar surroundings. He wondered, could this be Max. In fact it was Maxamillion, the large dog that he had lived on in a previous life.

Fergus had recognised the old area where he used to play swinging out. He saw the place where he, and Dwiddle laid rope traps in order to trip up older folk. What little terrors we must have been, thought Fergus.

Fergus was very happy now, as he had completed a full circle of life. He was back where he started as a child. Fergus was now a little older, there were a few grey hairs beginning to appear around his side burns. He also used a walking stick.

He still had a loving family, and lots of friends. He also thought that it would not be long before he would be a grandfather. His three sons were all madly in love with different females this time. "Thank the Lord". Said Fergus. Emma was completely out of the picture, but not forgotten. They could not help having regular mental flashes of a bygone beauty.

Fergus was having thoughts of days gone by, when he was too young to know better. He wondered where was his dear friend Dwiddle. He wondered what he would look like now. Would he look older. Has he got grey hair on his head, or has he got any hair at all. Is he married, does he have kids, perhaps he had left Max, and found a totally new life somewhere else.

He had hoped that he might run into him one day, it would be lovely to see him again, and exchange stories, he hoped Dwiddle was a reformed character by now.

Fergus was getting emotional, and very near to tears. All these questions would be answered in time.

Life looked very rosy for all, and at last a big smile was on Mr Fergus's face. He set about gathering together all his beloved family. He would show them all the old haunts he used to frequent as a tearaway youth. Fergus had tender feelings for Max. After all, he did provide food and lodgings for him, and all his little friends.

Fergus would now have to start a whole new community. There were lots of plans to be made, and he knew he would never be short of helpers. His vegetarian days were now over. A new and better life was just about to begin again for our little hero, and all his lovely family. Fergus and all his little friends were where all fleas belong. They were on a dog.

No one knew how many years had elapsed since Fergus had originally been forced off Max..

I hope you enjoyed this story of complete fable. God only knows how it got into my mind.

J.A.T.H.
2008

A Big Thanks To All Those
Who Lent A Hand
Especially Rose.
Also, Luke. Madelein. Toby. Ben.
Elisabeth Mc Dermot. Kim. Janine.
Amanda. Jodie. Emma. And Tracy.

John Healy was born in Dublin in 1935, but has lived in London for the past 50 years. He was a London Black Cab driver for 28 years until he retired in 2008. During this time many famous people sat in his cab including; Charlton Heston, Joan Collins, Jeffery Archer, George Best, Richard Branson and Judy Dench to name a few.

John has a son and a daughter who are twins and three grandchildren (two of whom appear as characters in the book!) Unfortunately John's dear wife Rose died in October 2008 of Motor Neurones disease, but Rose encouraged him to write this book and would have been very proud of his achievement.

John would like to thank the Motor Neurones Society for all their support.

LaVergne, TN USA
05 December 2009
1639LVUK00005BA